MEDITATION DECODED

UNDERSTANDING MEDITATION FOR BETTER RESULTS

RANJAN CHADHA

Thank you, Guru Maharaj Prem Rawat Ji for your benevolence and blessings. The gift of your Knowledge has helped me in making this effort.

CONTENTS

INTRODUCTION

In a fast-paced world filled with constant distractions and a never-ending stream of information, finding moments of peace and tranquillity is a challenge. Many of us yearn for a way to quiet our minds, alleviate stress, and connect with a deeper sense of self. This is where meditation comes in.

Welcome to *Meditation Decoded: Understanding Meditation for Better Results,* my Kindle book that aims to shed light on the transformative power of this ancient practice. Whether you're a beginner or someone seeking a deeper understanding of meditation, this book will serve as your invaluable companion on the journey to inner calm and self-discovery.

I am simply a practitioner who has been meditating for several years, and I believe it would be beneficial to share some of the insights I have gained. I intend to help you understand the transformative power of daily meditation and guide you on how to find a way out of the blockages you may encounter on your meditation journey, many of which I faced myself.

On 1 March 1972, I was bestowed with the gift of Knowledge, which included the techniques required for meditation, by Prem Rawat. At that time, he was known as Guru Maharaj Ji or Balyogeshwar Shri Sant Ji Maharaj.

However, in recent years, he has discarded the esoteric, mystical, and spiritual titles associated with those names and adopted a more inclusive and secular approach. He now prefers to be called Prem Rawat, his given name, although many still address him as Guru Maharaj Ji.

When I initially started practising meditation, I firmly believed that what I was receiving was unparalleled. I had profound experiences that surpassed my imagination. At that time, I felt no need to seek further lessons in meditation and I still feel the same way. However, after just three years, I became inconsistent with my practice and drifted away from it. Even though I would meditate oft and on I always had it in the back of my mind somewhere.

I questioned myself on this. Why did I drift away? Many years later it was explained to me by an experienced monk who was also initiated into the same Knowledge as I was. He said that such a behaviour is often exhibited by some people who start to meditate. He further elucidated it with a parable. 'When one starts to broom a room, it appears dirtier than before as the dust flies around and by just looking at the mess one is discouraged from cleaning it further. Then after sometime when the dust has settled and one relooks at the room it appears that the little cleaning done earlier did make the room cleaner.' He said that idea is that one should not be discouraged and give up. Restart and keep at it.

In 2003, I had moments of realization that urged me to commit to regular meditation practice. Since then, I have diligently practised it, and I am now convinced that if there is one skill we should learn, it is how to meditate. With that said, and without claiming to be an expert, I would like to share my thoughts and insights gained from meditation. Maybe these insights will help and inspire some to start meditating and others to continue on this path and practise meditation to get better results.

Throughout this book, whenever I refer to meditation, I am specifically referring to the meditation technique that I practise. I am not aware of any other techniques beyond my own. Nowadays, I come across various meditation techniques under different names. One commonly mentioned technique is known as 'witnessing the breath'. I have also used this term, primarily because it aligns with the research that I have quoted and resonates with most of my personal experiences.

Researchers who have published their findings often tell us that meditation in any form will sooner or later lead to some sort of inner calm. This may be true for physiological changes that the researchers so painstakingly record and corelate. However, we must remember that meditation goes way beyond the confines of research labs. Research serves only as a limited validation of the claims made by some as to what meditation can do to us physiologically.

However, if you feel that your present practice is not up to the mark or if you would like to learn the Knowledge of meditation, please feel free to contact Prem Rawat at www.premrawat.com OR www.wopg.org and learn more about him also at Timeless Today, https://www.timelesstoday.tv/.

In this book on meditation, we will explore the exact meaning of the phrase 'to meditate' and get a glimpse of the power of meditation. We will debunk common myths and clear some misconceptions about meditation. This little book will prove to be a valuable resource for anyone looking to develop a regular meditation practice.

Meditation is a simple yet powerful technique that involves focusing one's attention to achieve a state of calm and relaxation. Contrary to popular belief, meditation does not require a specific religious or spiritual affiliation. It can be practised by anyone, anywhere, and at any time.

We will dive into some of the reasons why meditation has become increasingly relevant in our modern lives. From reducing stress and anxiety to improving focus and enhancing creativity, meditation offers a multitude of benefits that extend far beyond your meditation cushion. We will explore the scientific research that supports these claims and highlight the profound impact that meditation can have on our overall quality of life. Numerous myths and misunderstandings often deter individuals from embarking on a meditation practice. Hopefully, the common misconceptions surrounding meditation will be dispelled. Debunking these myths and addressing widely believed concerns will remove the barriers that prevent one from fully embracing the transformative potential of meditation. Separating fact from fiction will help develop a clearer perspective on what meditation truly entails.

So, take a deep breath, find a comfortable space, and prepare to embark on a path of self-discovery and inner peace. Let *Meditation Decoded: Understanding Meditation for Better Results* be your inspiration as we unravel the mysteries of this transformative practice and unlock the immense potential within you.

How to Get Started with My Kindle Book on Meditation:

Getting started with my Kindle book on meditation is straightforward. Simply download the book from Amazon and start reading!

One of the most important things to remember when starting a meditation practice is to be patient and compassionate with yourself. Meditation is a skill that takes time and practice to develop, so it's important to approach it with a sense of curiosity and openness.

Chapter One

MEDITATION: BUSTING MYTHS

In the fall of 1971, at eighteen years old, I was studying economics at Sri Ram College of Commerce, Delhi University. A series of profound experiences that made me restless led me to seek the meaning behind my existence, beginning my exploration into consciousness and spirituality.

I once believed spirituality and religion were synonymous. It wasn't until I read *Autobiography of a Yogi* by Paramahansa Yogananda that I understood their distinct differences.

Religion and spirituality diverge in substantial ways. Religion consists of organized beliefs and outwardly practices shared by a community or group, while spirituality focuses on individual pursuits for inner peace and purpose. This peace often emerges from an enhanced comprehension and understanding of life, drawing insights from meditation.

However, the term 'spirituality' now encompasses various ideas and emotions, primarily linked to inner thoughts and worldviews that recognize more than meets the senses. This perspective acknowledges a deeper meaning within the universe's mechanics, human consciousness beyond brain impulses, and existence beyond the physical body.

The most accurate depiction of spirituality stems from its etymological roots. Spirituality comes from the Latin 'spiritus', meaning 'breath', signifying life. It shares a connection with Vedic (Sanskrit) and Buddhist definitions, wherein the word for breath is 'prana', symbolizing the life-giving essence and spirit.

My quest for the profound truths about our reality and the cosmos drove me to seek answers to age-old questions that have intrigued humankind for millennia. These eternal inquiries, also called the soul questions, delve deep into the core of our being, prompting us to ponder our identity, our purpose, and the essence of life. Traditional religions have failed to provide definitive solutions to these conundrums.

In an attempt to uncover the answers to these timeless questions, I sought inspiration from individuals who embarked on similar journeys. It soon became clear that mastering meditation was a crucial step in gaining access to these elusive truths since they resided within my consciousness rather than in external sources.

As a devotee of science, I was familiar with empirical research and with validation, where 'knowing' is a sensory activity and experience. I naively believed that scientific discovery would eventually reveal the answers to even these most persistent mysteries. However, spirituality challenged this presumption and instructed me to look inwards instead. Real knowing comes from within. Accepting this notion necessitated learning the art of meditation, marking another shift in my understanding and shattering a long-held belief.

The Vedas, ancient Indian scriptures that date back to 1500 BCE, contain the earliest meditation texts. The Upanishads, significant Vedic texts composed between 800 and400 BCE, elucidate the concepts of the self, the universe, and the merging of individual consciousness with the universal awareness for spiritual enlightenment. Meditation plays a vital role in this process.

Buddhism has an extensive meditation history as well; the Pali Canon, penned in the first century BCE, provides comprehensive guidelines for various meditation methods such as mindfulness and loving-kindness.

In essence, ancient Vedic and Buddhist scriptures highlight meditation's significance in attaining spiritual enlightenment and inner tranquillity. Meditation here is defined as an exercise of focusing attention on specific objects or thoughts to achieve clarity of mind and emotional stability, resulting in the integration of personal and universal consciousness. The term has expanded its reach into other secular realms for stress relief and enhancing mental and physical well-being.

The Ashtanga (an eight-limbed process) yoga founder, Sage Patanjali, penned the Yoga Sutras around 500 BCE. This ancient Sanskrit text comprises 196 brief statements called sutras, each guiding individuals towards achieving 'yoga'—a harmonious connection between personal and universal consciousness. The Ashtanga yoga system outlines eight essential steps:

1. Yama: Behavioural ethics and restraints
2. Niyama: Discipline and observances
3. Āsana: Steady and comfortable physical postures
4. Prāṇāyāma: Breath control
5. Pratyahara: Sensory withdrawal
6. Gyana: {Also called Dharna in some texts} Knowledge of meditational techniques
7. Dhyāna: Concentration
8. Samādhi: Total absorption

Originating from Vedic and Buddhist traditions, samādhi represents a meditative state characterized by deep focus, a stillness of the mind, and enhanced awareness, where a person experiences unity with their inner self and feels an interconnectedness with the cosmos. The samādhi experience greatly varies among individuals and traditions—some perceive it as blissful ecstasy, while others view it as profound wisdom.

Samādhi is a highly sophisticated state of consciousness that requires years of meditation practice and spiritual discipline for attainment. Many consider it the ultimate meditation goal—a gateway to elevated consciousness and spiritual awakening.

Within Semitic religions, such as Judaism, Christianity, and Islam, meditation and contemplation are present in the sacred texts and customs. In Judaism, Hitbodedut is a reflective prayer that encourages silent meditation and pondering the Torah's teachings. The Psalms are also seen as meditative passages expressing praise, gratitude, and a desire for God.

Christianity offers various meditation practices, including Lectio Divina, which focuses on scripture analysis and centring prayer, where a repeated word or phrase helps quiet the mind and concentrate on God. Renowned Christian mystics like St. John of the Cross and St. Teresa of Avila also provide insights into contemplative prayer.

In Islam, Sufism accentuates the significance of meditation and contemplation to attain a direct connection with God. Sufi rituals involve reciting particular phrases or mantras, called dhikr, and silent meditation, known as muraqaba.

Although meditation's role may differ across religions, many faiths contain references to meditation and contemplative acts in their sacred texts and practices. In Semitic religions, for example, meditation often conveys introspection rather than its Vedic or Buddhist interpretations—an endeavour to unite individual awareness with universal consciousness, thus making meditation and contemplation synonymous.

One of the recent religions in the world is Sikhism, and the spiritual tradition of Sikhism offers a wealth of depth and intricacy to explore. Rooted as it is in the Vedic tradition, it does not mince words in distinguishing between contemplation and meditation.

Meditation holds great importance in Sikhism, serving as a crucial component of spiritual growth and establishing a connection with the divine. The fundamental aspects of Sikh meditation include breath awareness and divine connection.

Breath awareness: Sikh meditative practices often involve directing attention to the breath, aiming to quiet the mind and enhance one's spiritual encounter. By focusing on the natural rhythm of their breath, Sikhs strive to develop mindfulness and inner tranquillity.

Divine connection: The ultimate objective of meditation in Sikhism is to establish a profound bond with the divine. Through regular meditation, Sikhs aspire to achieve a sense of unity with God, transcending the limitations of the ego and recognizing their authentic spiritual essence.

The word 'meditate' traces its roots to the Latin term 'meditatum', which means 'to ponder'. Monk Guigo II coined this expression in the twelfth century CE. This etymology led to some confusion regarding the term's meaning until recently.

Let's explore the sixth stage of Patanjali's Ashtanga yoga, the eight fold path of yoga, known as gyāna, a term denoting knowledge. In this phase, a master imparts essential wisdom to the students, instructing them on where and how to focus their attention. Following this is the seventh stage, called dhyāna, which means 'attention' as a noun and 'to pay attention' or 'to focus attention' as a verb. Here, the students practise the teachings received from their master. What is now commonly referred to as meditation stems from this act of focusing one's attention. Since there is no precise English equivalent for dhyāna, the term 'meditate' has replaced its original meaning of musing or reflecting on a subject.

It is evident that while contemplation involves deep thought and consideration, meditation empowers attention to maintain focus in a specific manner, ultimately connecting to universal consciousness—the very core of consciousness. Recognizing this distinction allows for greater clarity in our spiritual journey and emphasizes that meditation is irreplaceable in its benefits.

The wisdom of meditation, which dates back centuries, gained significant popularity in the Western world during the eighteenth century CE. The release of the Tibetan Book of the Dead in 1927 fascinated Western audiences and sparked a keen interest in meditative practices. This was later followed by the introduction of insight meditation, known as the Vipassana movement, originating in Burma in the 1950s. The publication of Jack Kerouac's *The Dharma Bums* in 1958 further amplified the greater public's interest in meditation. Finally, in 1979, the United States established the Mindfulness-Based Stress Reduction (MBSR) programme, integrating meditative techniques into treatment plans for patients suffering from chronic diseases.

Since then, various disciplines of study in human behaviour and well-being have adopted different techniques of meditation to study its effects on the human mind, brain, and body. Psychology, neuroscience of spirituality, neurobiology of spirituality, and neurotheology, to name a few, have redefined meditation while keeping its essence in place, to suit the objectives of their research. This has helped in shattering the myth that meditation is some kind of esoteric supernatural belief and practice. These studies have made many people aware that the knowledge and practice of meditation are secular and transcend all limitations of ethnicity and religious affiliations.

Chapter Two

TAMING THE MONKEY MIND: THE ONLY SKILL WE NEED

Why Should We Meditate?

We see the marvels of technology all around us, and there is absolutely no doubt that we have done amazing things. As humans, we have the most highly developed brains on this planet—the crown jewel of evolution. With these remarkable brains, we have shaped and reshaped this planet. We have examined the smallest atoms, contemplated the cosmos, ventured into space and explored everything in between.

However, when we look at some statistics, we realize that despite all the technological and scientific advances, we have never been more miserable as a species. Sometime back a survey that came out in America said that between 2015 and 2018, 13 per cent of Americans took antidepressants, and this percentage is growing. Mental health and emotional well-being issues have made psychiatry and psychotherapy big businesses not only in America but also the world over. Pharma companies are making billions selling psychotropic medicines.

Let us take a look at the most populated country in the world—India, the region that gave us the Vedas and meditation. Today, India is a major hub of the digital world, while simultaneously being high on poverty and hunger indices. The disparity between the Haves and the Have-nots is alarming. The statistics from India reveal a picture that is very similar to the one from the USA.

In 2017 one in every 20 Indians suffered from depression. Around 1 million more prescriptions for anti-depressants were written in 2016 in comparison to 2015, shows data collated by health information agencies. While 30.35 million prescriptions (for newly diagnosed patients) were written in 2015, doctors wrote 30.46 million new prescriptions in 2016.

In India we have at least 150,000–180,000 people who unfortunately die by suicide every year, many of them aged between fifteen and twenty-nine. In a recent survey, it was found that at least 40 per cent of people living in India and working in corporate India experience stress, anxiety, and depression. We just need to examine the numbers: road rage, homicide, violent crimes, divorce, isolation, and loneliness are all happening throughout India.

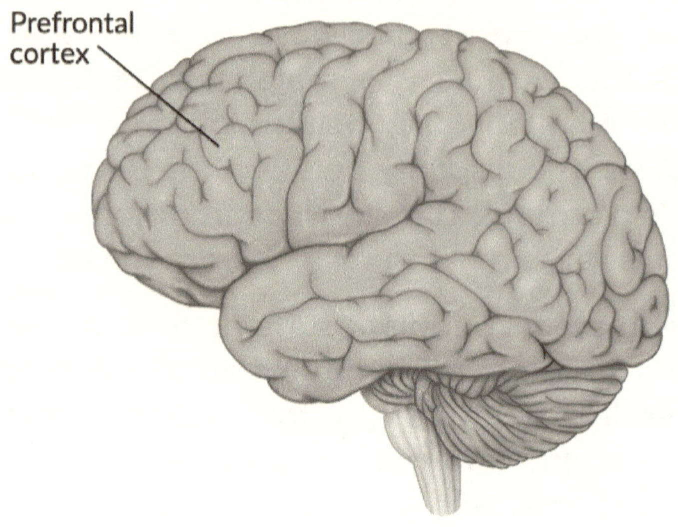

'The prefrontal cortex (PFC) intelligently regulates our thoughts, actions, and emotions through extensive connections with other brain regions The [PFC]—the most evolved brain region—subserves our highest-order cognitive abilities. The part of the brain that is key to reasoning, problem-solving, comprehension, impulse control, creativity, and perseverance. However, it is also the brain region that is most sensitive to the detrimental effects of stress exposure. Even quite mild but acutely uncontrollable stress can cause a rapid and dramatic loss of prefrontal cognitive abilities, and more prolonged stress exposure causes architectural changes in prefrontal dendrites. 2{a} (Quoted from 'Stress signalling pathways that impair prefrontal cortex structure and function' by Amy F. T. Arnsten.)

Here arises a fundamental question: Why is it that despite our remarkable advancements and achievements, we often find ourselves engulfed in suffering? Could it be that the very source of our progress and development is also the wellspring of our pain and anguish?

Our brain, truly unique in its capabilities, harbours a distinct region known as the prefrontal cortex. It is the grey matter of the anterior part of the frontal lobe that is highly developed in humans and plays a role in the regulation of complex cognitive, emotional, and behavioural functioning. *As Amy F.T. Arnsten says in the paper 'Stress signalling pathways that impair prefrontal cortex structure and function': 'The prefrontal cortex (PFC) intelligently regulates our thoughts, actions, and emotions through extensive connections with other brain regions. The prefrontal cortex—the most evolved brain region—subserves our highest-order cognitive abilities. The part of the brain that is key to reasoning, problem-solving, comprehension, impulse control, creativity, and perseverance.*

'However, it is also this region of the brain that is most sensitive to the detrimental effects of stress exposure. Even quite mild but acutely uncontrollable stress can cause a rapid and dramatic loss of prefrontal cognitive abilities, and more prolonged stress exposure causes architectural changes in prefrontal dendrites.'

This segment of the brain surpasses those found in any other species in terms of sophistication and development, affording us the extraordinary ability to communicate verbally, among other things. Just consider the wonder of an idea originating in my mind, transforming into vibrations carried through the air, and ultimately reaching your brain as interpreted sound. It's truly remarkable what our brains are capable of achieving.

It is through this extraordinary brain that we transcend the capriciousness of the natural environment. We possess the capacity to pause, to think, and to envision the future. Our brains can be likened to virtual reality machines, enabling us to contemplate multiple potential realities and make life decisions. This unique attribute has propelled our species to unparalleled achievements.

However, these advanced faculties also possess a darker aspect. It is through this very brain that, while you read these words, your mind may wander elsewhere, pondering the allure of a more captivating Netflix movie or other distractions, like checking out messages on your phone to see if so-and-so has replied or initiated a new conversation. The list can be long.

The mind, it seems, is trapped in an endless cycle of comparison, constantly questioning, 'What's happening here?' and 'What could it be?' Our brain seems almost fixated on the inquiries of 'Who am I?' and 'What is my story?' as well as 'What is occurring in my life at this moment?' The brain persistently assesses whether the present aligns with our narrative or if we desire a different outcome. It is this facet of our brain that engenders dissatisfaction as we perpetually compare our lives. We attain a desirable job, relishing it for a time, but soon yearn for more—a promotion, perhaps. We enter into marriage, yet find it arduous to escape the clutches of this incessant comparison, this ceaseless mental chatter. It often goes on like 'Did I make the right choice?', or 'Could I have had a happier life with someone else?', or even 'Perhaps the first one I saw and wanted to marry would have been a better choice!', and on and on.

The funny thing about this brain is that it's not interested in our happiness; it's not interested in our fulfilment. It's only interested in our survival and our sense of significance. This part of the brain gives us awareness, and it lets us know that we are born, that we are here for a limited time, and that we are going to die. A remarkable, almost terrible predicament for us as human beings, isn't it? Because no other animal species is subject to that kind of awareness.

Unlike other animals, we humans possess a unique capability: the ability to dwell in the present moment and pretend otherwise. Consider a hypothetical dog in your midst—it would either attentively observe you or depart. It wouldn't feign interest. However, this ability of ours to feign interest or detach oneself from the present has its drawbacks. One of the main drawbacks is that it leads to a disconnection from reality. We can become so engrossed in our fantasies, worries, or regrets that we lose touch with the present moment and the experiences unfolding right in front of us. This detachment can hinder our ability to fully engage with others, appreciate the beauty of our surroundings, and experience life to its fullest.

Deep within our brains lies the amygdala, a primitive structure that has evolved over millions of years and is shared among mammals. *The amygdala is responsible for perceiving emotions such as anger, fear, and sadness, as well as controlling aggression. The amygdala helps store memories of events and feelings so that an individual may recognize similar events in the future. The amygdala is commonly thought to form the core of a neural system for processing fearful and threatening stimuli, including the detection of threats and activation of appropriate fear-*

related behaviours in response to threatening or dangerous stimuli.

This crucial component ensures our survival. Interestingly, certain conditions and diseases can lead to the atrophy and eventual demise of the amygdala. In such cases, fear dissipates entirely, which may seem appealing. Living without fear—sounds good!

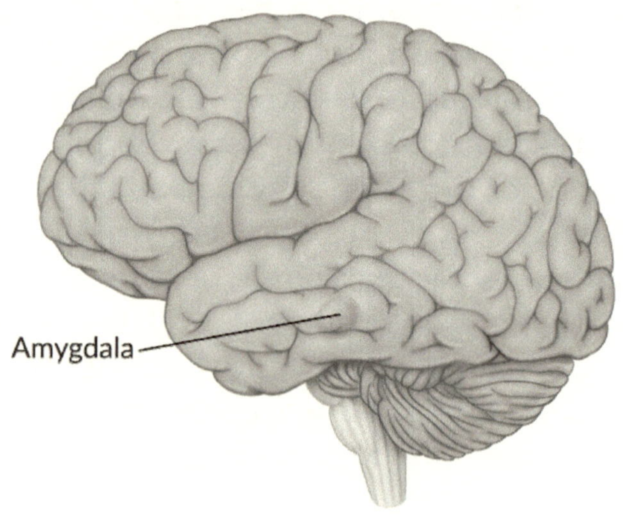

The amygdala is responsible for perceiving emotions such as anger, fear, and sadness, as well as controlling aggression. The amygdala helps store memories of events and feelings so that an individual may recognize similar events in the future. The amygdala is commonly thought to form the core of a neural system for processing fearful and threatening stimuli, 2{c} including the detection of threats and activation of appropriate fear-related behaviours in response to threatening or dangerous stimuli. (Material from 'Facing the role of the amygdala in emotional information processing' by Mark G. Baxter and Paula L. Croxson.)

Yet, fear serves an essential purpose. It is a protective mechanism, alerting us to potential threats and enabling us to safeguard ourselves. When animals face danger, they instinctively respond by fighting or fleeing. Nevertheless, their response is purely in defence of their physical well-being. Threats to an animal imply a direct assault on its physical self. In contrast, the human amygdala has assumed a profoundly different role. It now safeguards not only our physical being but also our sense of identity and emotional self, which are essentially mere thoughts and beliefs. Thus, when our boss regards us with an odd expression or our significant other fails to return a call, the amygdala is triggered, evoking a sense of threat and emotional distress.

By implication, presently, we exist in a realm of beliefs rather than reality. As you read these words, your perception extends beyond mere visual and cognitive reception. We are present not only in the physical world but also in the realm within our mind—a world we strive to protect, sometimes even more than our physical being. Strangely, humans are the only species willing to kill or sacrifice their lives for beliefs, which are essentially abstract thoughts in our minds. Nevertheless, we are prepared to make such extreme sacrifices because our beliefs hold immense significance for us; they are the driving force behind our aspirations and desires. When our envisioned mental constructs deviate from the course of reality, we experience distress, as we yearn to hold on to our cherished notions.

Regrettably, we often forget that life resembles a flowing river composed of continuous moments. It proceeds ceaselessly, indifferent to our narratives or stories. Yet, despite its inherent fluidity, we attempt to obstruct and compartmentalize this river. It is akin to refusing its natural course, trying to halt its flow exclusively for our benefit. We crave control over its direction, demanding that events unfold according to our desires.

Consequently, when favourable circumstances transpire, we embrace them tightly, fearing their loss. On the other hand, when adversity strikes, we instinctively seek to evade it. Thereby, we never truly exist in the present moment, fully immersed in life as it unfolds. Instead, we are trapped in a perpetual cycle of oscillating between past and future, safeguarding our beliefs. This way of life is both irrational and unsustainable, shackling us to an existence marked by constant turmoil.

So where does meditation fit in? Meditation serves as a means to gain mastery over our remarkably intricate and complex brains.

Curiously, this essential knowledge to gain mastery over our remarkably intricate and complex brains eludes us in the confines of traditional schooling. In school, we were inundated with facts and figures, our minds serving as mere repositories for the information imparted to us. Yet, we were never taught how to wield this incredible tool, much like possessing a finely honed instrument capable of cutting and dissecting without understanding its purpose or how to utilize it effectively. Our mind, too, possesses this tremendous capacity, yet we remain unaware of how to harness its potential. Unaware of our power over it, our mind, much like a sharp instrument, occasionally stabs us, inflicting pain that we mistakenly attribute to life's inherent suffering. Thus, meditation entails comprehending that our mind, this sharp and extraordinary instrument, should indeed be under our control. Failing to learn how to master our mind means surrendering to its whims and caprices.

Meditation, undoubtedly, provides the necessary path that leads to seizing control of our brains. Abundant evidence supports its efficacy in this regard. Meditation is a powerful practice that nurtures and supports the natural and optimal functioning of our brain. Numerous studies provide compelling evidence of its positive effects. By engaging in meditation, we bring balance to the prefrontal cortex, reduce amygdala activity, harmonize the left and right hemispheres of the brain, and enhance our immune system. Furthermore, research has explored the correlation between meditation and decreased blood pressure and the potential for reducing the activation of cancer-related genes, which could potentially lower the risk of developing cancer.

Beyond these physiological benefits, meditation offers profound insights into our true selves and our deepest desires. It equips us with the ability to navigate the chaos, unrest, confusion, and desires that arise from the incessant chatter of our minds, which prevents us from living a harmonious and peaceful life free from the burden of stress. It empowers us to utilize our brains to contemplate the past and to plan the future when necessary, while also granting us the invaluable capacity to pause, observe, and find tranquillity amidst the storm. Once we discover and connect with this inner stillness, we can carry it with us wherever we go, akin to the calm eye of a storm or the centre of a cyclone.

There are various meditation techniques available, but perhaps one of the most commonly employed, especially for scientific research, is known as the 'witnessing the breath' technique. Breathing holds a unique position among bodily functions as it can be consciously controlled or left to operate unconsciously.

The region of the brain responsible for managing crucial functions like blood pressure, heart rate, and digestion also oversees our breathing, which is why we typically don't need to consciously think about it. However, upon closer examination, we discover that our breath is intricately intertwined with our emotions. When we experience stress, our breath tends to constrict, while relaxation brings forth gentle and easy breathing. Additionally, anger often manifests as sharp and shallow breaths. Our breath is deeply connected to the unconscious realm of our brain, which governs our emotional state, sense of self, and overall mood.

Engaging in conscious breathing provides us with an opportunity to establish a connection with the unconscious part of our brain. Through the practice of witnessing the breath, we employ our conscious mind to observe and bear witness to the subtle workings of our unconscious mind. Reflecting on this interplay between our conscious and unconscious selves is truly remarkable and an awe-inspiring phenomenon.

EXPLODING MISCONCEPTIONS

Chapter Three

I CANNOT SIT STILL FOR LONG

How Do I Sit for So Long During A Meditation Session?

To meditate well, we need to have the ability to sit comfortably in one position for at least twenty minutes, though an hour is ideal.

Most people have this grandiose idea of a 'correct way' to sit while meditating. All meditations, sooner or later, lead to the same goal—a greater sense of inner peace and happiness—but some practices will allow our daily meditation to feel a lot easier. By the grandiose idea, I mean impersonating a monk or a saint and then not being able to sit for long in any monk-like position with comfort. The thought 'I can't sit for long' is just a misconception and a myth of our own making.

Many people turn to meditation as a way to relieve stress and anxiety, and improve overall well-being. It's a simple practice that requires nothing more than a comfortable sitting position. It can be practised by anyone, wearing anything and having any kind of look. However, some people take the idea of the 'right' posture too far and try to mimic the traditional lotus position used by monks and saints. Unfortunately, this can be counterproductive, as discomfort or pain can prevent you from achieving a deep meditative state. That is why posturing as a monk to meditate doesn't work. It can hurt and prevent meditation. There is a need to disassociate meditation from sainthood.

The Problem with The Lotus Position

The lotus position involves crossing your legs with your feet on top of your thighs, while your hands rest on your knees or lap. While it may look peaceful and serene, it can be quite uncomfortable for most people, especially if they're not used to sitting in that position for extended periods. Your hips and knees can start to ache, your back may feel strained, and your feet can go numb. All of these distractions can make it difficult to focus and quieten the mind, which are the main goals of meditation.

There are alternatives to sitting in the lotus position. But even these can be uncomfortable for most who lack the required flexibility and practice. The alternatives that can be considered include:

The Burmese Position

This position involves sitting cross-legged with one foot in front of the other and the hands resting on the knees. It's a bit easier on the hips and knees than the lotus position and still allows for a good posture.

The Seiza Position

In this position, sit on your heels with your legs folded underneath you and your hands resting on your thighs. A cushion to elevate the hips may be used if needed. This position takes some pressure off the knees and ankles and can be easier on the back.

The Chair Position

If sitting on the floor isn't an option, you can still meditate in a chair. Just make sure you sit up straight with your feet flat on the ground and your hands resting in your lap. Choose a chair with a straight back and avoid leaning back or slouching.

Throughout our lives, most of us have become accustomed to sitting on chairs. As a result, our muscles and joints have adapted to finding comfort exclusively in this sitting position. Therefore, it takes practice and adjustment to be able to sit on the floor in monk-like or other positions for extended periods. When beginners attempt to meditate in an uncomfortable position, it can feel as though they are grappling with their own thoughts and mental restlessness. It's not surprising that such an experience may leave them feeling that meditation is too challenging and not worth their time and effort.

Instead of forcing yourself into positions commonly seen in photos of people meditating, it is advisable to prioritize comfort while sitting. You can use back support and pillows if necessary. The remarkable thing is that your body becomes a non-distracting element in the meditation process. If you are new to meditation, you can even sit in a relaxed manner as if you were watching your favourite television show. By sitting comfortably and practising your meditation you will discover experiences that are significantly more profound than anything you have encountered before. The key is to practise consistently.

Meditation is not about how we sit, where we sit, or what posture we sit in. Meditation is about focus—focusing your attention on the breath or whatever it is you have chosen to meditate upon and thus observing your monkey mind do its jumps.

Chapter Four

I CANNOT SUPPRESS MY THOUGHTS

The need to suppress one's thoughts is not a prerequisite to meditation. Ample research on the subject suggests otherwise. That is, if we don't suppress our thoughts, we get a better meditative experience.

When we make an active effort to suppress specific thoughts, they resurface more frequently in our minds. This psychological phenomenon is known as the ironic process theory, which can have significant implications for both our performance inside and outside of the boxing ring, so to speak.

But what exactly is the ironic process theory? It is a psychological concept, also referred to as the white bear problem, that suggests our deliberate attempts to suppress thoughts make them more likely to emerge.

This theory was first explored by social psychologist Daniel Wegner in 1987 during his study on thought suppression. Through his research, Wegner discovered that individuals instructed not to think about a white bear became more aware of the idea they were trying to suppress. This realization led to the understanding that suppressing thoughts can have paradoxical effects, potentially resulting in an obsessive or intrusive thinking pattern.

In the experiment conducted by Wegner, a group of people were asked to conjure up a white bear in their imagination and then focus on this mental picture for five minutes. Afterwards, they were instructed to spend another five minutes avoiding any thoughts about the white bear. Surprisingly, when they were supposed to imagine and focus on the white bear, they reported that their minds would drift off to other thoughts. Conversely, when they were not supposed to be thinking about the white bear, it occupied most of their thoughts, with some individuals bordering on obsession. This study drew two important conclusions:

- If you focus on anything for around five or six seconds, your mind naturally tends to divert to unrelated thoughts.
- Trying to suppress your thoughts ultimately leads to an increase in the thoughts you try to avoid.

Therefore, suppressing thoughts does not lead to a positive outcome in terms of meditation or mental well-being.

If suppressing thoughts during meditation doesn't yield positive results, what happens when we allow the mind to wander?

Research has been conducted on numerous meditation techniques, such as mindfulness, Zen, Acem, meditation drumming, chakra, Buddhist, and transcendental meditation. Despite their differences, these techniques share a common goal: to cultivate inner peace, reduce stress, improve focus, enhance self-awareness, and aid in the processing of thoughts and emotions.

Choosing the right meditation technique can be overwhelming for those seeking solace from overwhelming stress. Historically, scientific research in this field has been limited, but that is changing.

A team of researchers from the Norwegian University of Science and Technology (NTNU), the University of Oslo, and the University of Sydney has been actively investigating how different types of meditation affect the brain. Their findings, published in the journals *Frontiers in Human Neuroscience* and *Science Daily*, shed light on what happens when we allow the mind to wander.

Meditation techniques can be broadly categorized into two groups: concentrative meditation and nondirective meditation.

In concentrative meditation, practitioners focus their attention on specific thoughts while deliberately suppressing other distractions. Nondirective meditation, on the other hand, involves effortlessly concentrating on the breath or a meditation sound, allowing the mind to freely wander. Several contemporary meditation methods fall into the category of nondirective meditation.

While these nondirective meditation techniques are ancient, studies on them commenced about a decade ago. Unlike the white bear method of suppression, these meditation styles allow practitioners to let their minds drift and wander from one thought to the next.

In a research study, a group of fourteen individuals experienced in Acem meditation, a Norwegian technique, underwent MRI scans. They engaged in both nondirective meditation and a more focused concentrative meditation task during the scans. Participants with prior meditation experience were specifically selected to minimize confusion regarding the instructions during the MRI session.

The MRI scans revealed that nondirective meditation triggered higher brain activity in the region responsible for processing self-related thoughts and emotions compared to the resting state. In contrast, concentrative meditation showed activity in this brain area similar to that during rest.

Lead researcher Jian Xu expressed surprise at these findings, noting that the brain exhibited greater activity when thoughts wandered freely rather than when focused concentration was applied. This heightened activity occurs in the brain's resting network, associated with processing thoughts and emotions. Nondirective meditation demonstrated the most significant activation within this network.

Neuroscientist Svend Davanger, a co-author of the study, emphasized that nondirective meditation allows for more extensive processing of memories and emotions compared to concentrative meditation. The brain's resting network, which is most active during rest, becomes even more stimulated during nondirective meditation.

Davanger highlighted the significance of this brain area, describing it as a fundamental operating system or resting network that takes precedence when external tasks do not demand attention. He found it remarkable that a mental activity like nondirective meditation triggers higher activity in this network compared to regular rest.

In the book The Power of the Wandering Mind: *Nondirective Meditation in Science and Philosophy,* edited by Halvor Eifring, experts in neuroscience, medicine, psychology, philosophy, and the humanities share groundbreaking perspectives on how nondirective meditation interacts with the brain, mind, and culture.

In simpler terms, the study discovered that by allowing thoughts to shift freely from one to another during meditation, the mind engages in extensive mental and emotional processing. Interestingly, a wandering mind promotes a state of restfulness, activating a network responsible for deep relaxation, surpassing the level achieved during sleep at night. Sitting comfortably and meditating while letting the mind wander leads to bodily relaxation, and enhances mental organization and efficiency. Consequently, the thoughts experienced during meditation are not hindrances. Instead, they are symptomatic of the mind working on autopilot and are indications that the mind is subconsciously addressing the challenges faced in life. In other words, trying to control or suppress thoughts is also a stressful activity and a hindrance to the goals of meditation.

PRIORITIZING STILLNESS: THE ART OF DAILY MEDITATION

I Can't Find the Time to Meditate!

In our fast-paced, modern world, finding time for stillness and introspection seems like an ever-elusive dream. We often find ourselves caught in the whirlwind of responsibilities and obligations. This convinces us that we don't have time to meditate. Nevertheless, it is precisely during these hectic times that we need to prioritize moments of calm and clarity. As the old Zen saying goes, 'You should sit in meditation for twenty minutes every day, unless you're too busy. Then you should sit for an hour.'

Embracing The Zen Saying

At first sight, this Zen saying seems counterintuitive. How is it even possible for us to find more time in our busy schedules to meditate for an hour? On second thought, in typical Zenspeak, the profound wisdom of this saying lies in its encouragement to prioritize stillness and inner peace amidst the chaos of our lives.

Unveiling Clarity

When we are overwhelmed with tasks and responsibilities, it is easy to lose sight of our priorities and become entangled in a web of busyness. However, by committing to a longer meditation session during these periods, we gain the opportunity to unravel our thoughts, find clarity, and see through the fog of our daily lives. This time committed to meditation allows our minds to settle, which in turn enables us to approach our challenges with renewed energy and purpose.

Nurturing Well-Being

Our busyness and hectic schedules often prevent us from looking after ourselves and our well-being. We get used to stress and anxiety, and notice them only when we are on the brink of burnout. This affects our mental, emotional, and physical health. Meditation, when practised for twenty minutes or more, offers a respite from these propensities. Meditation calms the mind, soothes the nervous system, and restores balance within us. By prioritizing meditation, which is the only essential self-care practice, we are devoting time to our overall well-being, thus creating a solid foundation to handle the demands of daily life.

Shifting Perspectives

The Zen saying challenges our notions of time, busyness, and having a tight schedule. It invites us to question whether our perceived lack of time is merely a reflection of misplaced priorities and procrastination. For many, busyness becomes an excuse to avoid meditation. We need to rearrange this perspective of not having sufficient time and understanding the value of stillness. By embracing the paradoxical approach of dedicating more time to meditation when we feel most pressed for it, we embark on a transformative journey towards self-discovery and personal growth.

Thus, in a world that constantly demands our attention and energy, the importance of daily meditation cannot be overstated. The Zen saying reminds us that when life becomes overwhelmingly busy, that is precisely the moment when we need meditation the most. By making a conscious effort to set aside time for stillness, we nourish our minds, bodies, and souls. So, let us embrace the wisdom of the old Zen masters, setting aside at least twenty minutes each day to meditate, and if time permits, extending it to an hour. In doing so, we pave the way for a more balanced, meaningful, and fulfilled existence.

Time Refunded

Have you heard of time being refunded!? Believe me when I tell you there's only one activity that I'm aware of that will refund you the time you spent doing it and that's daily meditation.

Here is what I mean by that. We possess two distinct measures of age: chronological age and biological age. Chronological age refers to the number of years that have passed since birth, while the overall health and condition of our body tissues determine biological age. If exposed to excessive physiological or psychological stress, our biological age can exceed our chronological age significantly. A notable example is Dr Martin Luther King Jr, who passed away at the age of thirty-nine. Upon conducting an autopsy, his body resembled that of a sixty-year-old, indicating a biological age that surpassed his chronological age by over twenty years due to the immense stress and pressure he endured.

In recent decades, research has uncovered the potential of meditation to slow the process of biological ageing. This essentially means that if an individual's chronological and biological ages were aligned at the age of thirty, and they began practising daily meditation, by the time they reached thirty-five, their skin elasticity, sexual responsiveness, vision, memory, and auditory threshold would resemble that of a twenty-three-year-old version of themselves. Consequently, their biological age would be seven years younger than when they started meditating. One of the most powerful tools to slow down the rate of ageing is meditation.

So saying I don't have time to meditate is akin to saying, I don't have time to file my tax refund where I was going to get back half of the money that I paid out.

While there is no magic potion to turn back the clock on ageing, scientists now have a reasonably good understanding of how the ageing process works, and what can be done to slow it down. An expanding body of evidence indicates that even fifteen minutes of daily meditation can effectively decelerate the ageing process, particularly at the cellular level.

Another study, conducted by a team of researchers from France and the United States, examined immune system cells from thirty-eight people. Of these, eighteen were regular meditators and twenty were not. The researchers used a process called DNA methylation to measure the epigenetic clock, a marker of ageing in cells.

They found that among the non-meditators, those who were fifty-two years and older had faster epigenetic clocks than the younger non-meditators. Meditators, on the other hand, did not show this same acceleration of the epigenetic clock. Older meditators with more years of meditation experience had slower epigenetic clocks. The researchers believe that chronic stress may speed up the epigenetic clock and that meditation, which is an effective way to reduce stress, can help slow down the ageing process.

Overall, the evidence suggests that meditation is a simple and effective way to slow down the ageing process. For those looking for ways to stay healthy and youthful, meditation is the best option. Thus, it is easy to see how daily meditation refunds the time spent on meditation.

Chapter Six

GAUGING PROGRESS IN MEDITATION

How Do I Know I Am Making Progress in My Meditation?

I used to wonder if I was making progress with my meditation practice. With regular and persistent meditation, as I began to feel greater inner peace and tranquillity, it dawned on me that in the realm of meditation, as it is often said, there is no specific goal to be achieved or a destination to arrive at—the journey of meditation is the essence, the goal, and the destination all at once. This viewpoint is contrary to the conventional idea of success, which is defined as achieving specific goals. Here we will explore the idea that the journey of meditation is self-contained and inherently meaningful, independent of any external achievements.

Meditation is a deeply personal and introspective practice that brings about multifarious benefits. These include, among others, increased mindfulness, reduced stress, and improved physiological and psychological well-being. Most of us believe that the sole criterion that marks success in meditation is the stillness of the mind. This belief is misleading. In reality, success in meditation goes beyond the absence of thoughts. Whereas self-awareness and personal experiences are crucial in evaluating the effectiveness of a meditative practice, let us see if progress in meditation can be gauged effectively.

Redefining Success in Meditation

It is erroneous to believe that success in meditation lies in achieving a completely still mind. To be able to comprehend success in meditation, redefining the concept of success becomes essential. Meditation is not about suppressing or eliminating thoughts but rather focusing on developing a non-judgemental awareness of the present moment. The ability to observe thoughts and emotions without getting entangled in them is one facet of what we can understand as success in meditation. With regular and consistent meditation, this ability inculcates in us a sense of inner peace and tranquillity.

Developing Self-Awareness

As we embark on the journey of meditation, we develop the capacity for self-awareness. Through mindful observation, we become attuned to the fluctuations of our thoughts, emotions, and sensations. This heightened self-awareness enables us to recognize patterns, attachments, and conditioned responses that may have been unconscious. By shedding light on these aspects of ourselves, we gain a deeper understanding of our true nature and begin to unravel the layers that veil our authentic selves.

Another way to gauge progress in meditation is by observing the levels of our self-awareness. By observing the patterns of our thoughts and emotions during meditation, we can gain insights into our mental and emotional states. We need to notice the frequency and intensity of our thoughts, the duration of our attention span, and our level of emotional reactivity. Over time, positive shifts, such as increased clarity, decreased mental chatter, and improved emotional regulation, will come to light.

Cultivating Mindfulness in Daily Life

The benefits of meditation extend beyond the meditation cushion. Mindfulness, the practice of being fully present in the moment, is a natural outcome of regular meditation. As mindfulness gets incorporated into our daily lives, we will see a change in our interactions, productivity, and overall well-being. We can notice that we have become more attentive, focused, and compassionate towards ourselves and others. These subtle changes indicate progress in the meditation practice.

Embracing The Present Moment

Meditation invites us to embrace the present moment and to be fully immersed in the here and now. Rather than fixating on the past or longing for the future, the practice of meditation teaches us to cultivate a deep appreciation for the present moment's richness and immediacy. In this way, every breath, every sensation, and every thought become an integral part of the journey, allowing us to connect with the essence of our being.

Cultivating Inner Transformation

The journey of meditation is a transformative process that takes place within. It is not about seeking external validation or striving for specific outcomes. Instead, it is a journey of inner exploration and growth. Through sustained practice, we cultivate qualities such as compassion, equanimity, and wisdom. We learn to navigate the complexities of our inner panorama with greater ease, embracing the challenges and growth opportunities that arise along the way.

Physical And Emotional Well-Being

Meditation has been linked to numerous physical and emotional benefits, such as reduced stress, improved sleep, and enhanced emotional resilience. With regular and consistent meditation, positive changes in physical health, such as lowered blood pressure, improved digestion, or reduced muscle tension, start to appear. Similarly, noticeable are experiences of greater emotional balance, increased self-compassion, or improved relationships. These indicators reflect progress in the meditation practice.

The Role of Feedback

Self-awareness is vital in gauging progress, but feedback from others can also provide valuable insights. Sometimes, people close to us may notice positive changes in our demeanour, attitude, or behaviour that we may not immediately recognize. They may observe in us an increased calmness, improved listening skills, or enhanced empathy. It is important to remain open to constructive feedback, as it can serve as a valuable external gauge of your progress in meditation.

Finding Stillness Amidst the Chaos

In our fast-paced and chaotic world, meditation provides an oasis of stillness and tranquillity. The journey of meditation allows us to develop an inner sanctuary, a place of refuge, regardless of external circumstances. It is through this practice that we discover the timeless wisdom that resides within us—a wisdom that remains unperturbed by the fluctuations of life. In this stillness, we connect with a deeper sense of peace and clarity, irrespective of the outcomes or circumstances we encounter.

Embracing Non-Attachment

In meditation, we learn to let go of attachments and expectations. We release the need for specific outcomes and surrender to the unfolding of the present moment. By relinquishing attachment, we free ourselves from the burden of striving and craving, allowing us to fully immerse ourselves in the journey without being hindered by preconceived notions of success or failure. This non-attachment opens the door to profound liberation and a sense of interconnectedness with all that is.

Embracing The Journey, Not the Destination

Lastly, it is crucial to remember that meditation is a lifelong practice, and progress is not linear. There will be days when your mind feels more restless, and thoughts seem to arise more frequently. The key is to cultivate an attitude of non-judgement and acceptance towards your meditation experiences. Instead of fixating on the assumed end goal of a completely still mind, the idea is to focus on the process of deepening self-awareness and fostering a greater sense of inner peace.

Thus, gauging progress in meditation is a deeply personal endeavour. It is not solely determined by the stillness of the mind but rather by being self-aware and mindful in daily life.

By embracing the journey of meditation and acknowledging the subtle shifts within ourselves, we can recognize the progress we have made, even if it may not always be immediately apparent. Remember that meditation is a lifelong practice, and each moment of presence and self-awareness contributes to your overall growth and well-being.

In the vast expanse of meditation, there is no external goal to be achieved or destination to arrive at. The journey of meditation is a transformative process that unfolds within, embracing the present moment, cultivating self-awareness, and fostering inner growth. It is a journey that invites us to find stillness amidst the chaos and embrace non-attachment. Ultimately, the journey itself becomes the destination—a profound exploration of our inner panorama, leading us to a deeper understanding of ourselves and how interconnected we are with all there is.

Chapter Seven

THE ILLUSION OF MEDITATION AS THE PANACEA

In recent years, meditation has gained immense popularity as a practice that promises to bring peace, tranquillity, and solutions to our problems. From self-help gurus to social media influencers, there seems to be an army of enthusiasts evangelizing about the transformative powers of meditation. Despite all their promises and popularity, it is important to view this phenomenon through the right lens and recognize that meditation, while undoubtedly beneficial, is not a magical panacea that can by itself instantly solve all of life's challenges. To say that it is a cure-all is an expression of ignorance and displays a lack of proper perspective on meditation. Let us explore and shed light on the reality behind the hype.

The Allure of Meditation

Meditation, in its essence, is a valuable tool for self-reflection and inner exploration. It offers a space for individuals to cultivate mindfulness, enhance focus, and attain a sense of inner calm. With its origins deeply rooted in ancient wisdom traditions, meditation has a rich history of helping people navigate the complexities of life. It is no wonder that many are drawn to its promise of alleviating stress, improving mental health, and even unlocking spiritual insights.

The Limitations of Meditation

While meditation can undoubtedly bring numerous benefits, it is essential to understand that it is not an instant cure-all for the myriad problems we face in our lives. It does not possess the power to simply erase our troubles or miraculously transform our circumstances. Instead, meditation invites us to cultivate a new perspective and relationship with our challenges. It teaches us to observe our thoughts and emotions without judgement, but it does not guarantee the overnight disappearance of these thoughts and emotions altogether.

Meditation And Real-Life Challenges

In our daily lives, we encounter many challenges that meditation by itself cannot resolve. It cannot mend broken relationships or resolve financial difficulties. Nevertheless, meditation inspires clarity, which leads to better understanding. It is this better understanding that reveals a way out for resolving issues that at first seemed extremely hard to resolve.

Talking Of Issues That at First Seemed Extremely Hard to Resolve

Research published by the Harvard Medical School has shown that meditation can be a complement to professional help when facing mental health issues, including depression, and can provide clarity when looking to make critical life decisions. Choosing a career, pursuing an education, choosing a life partner, managing finances, and taking calculated risks are just a few of the major critical life decisions we face in life.

Here, it is crucial to approach meditation with a balanced understanding, recognizing that meditation is not a quick-fix solution to mental health issues. After all, when you have barely meditated in your life, you cannot expect results from meditation overnight. Let us look at treating depression. Antidepressants and psychotherapy are the usual first-line treatments. However, ongoing research has suggested that regular meditation practice over time can help by changing how the brain responds to stress and anxiety.

The Danger of Spiritual Bypassing

One of the potential pitfalls associated with the exaggerated claims about meditation is spiritual bypassing. Spiritual bypassing refers to using spiritual practices as a means to avoid or bypass the uncomfortable aspects of our human experience. True meditative growth inspires and leads to a holistic approach that combines inner exploration with practical, real-life solutions.

The Balanced Approach

Meditation is a very potent tool for self-discovery, personal growth, and managing stress. Even so, it is important to adopt a balanced approach to its potential. Meditation can provide us with respite from the chaos of life, allowing us to cultivate mindfulness and gain clarity. This clarity attained through meditation will lead to the right understanding of our problems and issues as well as their solutions. The solutions may be in the form of adopting supportive strategies, such as seeking help when needed, taking action to address challenges, or engaging in healthy relationships with others.

Meditation is a dynamic practice that can bring numerous benefits to our lives. Then again, we must guard against the illusion that by itself it holds an immediate solution to all our problems. By approaching meditation with a realistic perspective, we can harness its transformative potential. True growth and well-being inspire clarity and the understanding to undertake a multifaceted approach, one that combines the wisdom of meditation with proactive engagement in our lives.

Meditation is not the panacea, but it can be a valuable part of a holistic approach to living a balanced and fulfilling life.

Chapter Eight

MEDITATION AND THE NON-JUDGEMENTAL ATTITUDE OF ACCEPTANCE

Throughout this book, I have used the term 'non-judgemental attitude of acceptance'. What exactly does this mean?

Meditation is a practice that encompasses fostering mindfulness, self-awareness, and inner peace. Central to meditation is the cultivation of a non-judgemental attitude of acceptance. This mindset is fundamental to the practice of meditation, which has gained significant popularity due to its therapeutic and stress-reduction benefits. Let's explore how meditation teaches us to adopt this non-judgemental attitude of acceptance and why it is valuable.

Observing Without Evaluation:

Meditation encourages individuals to observe their thoughts, feelings, bodily sensations, and external environment without attaching judgements or labels to them. This means acknowledging thoughts and emotions as they arise, without categorizing them as 'good' or 'bad', 'right' or 'wrong'. By doing so, meditation helps us become aware of the constant stream of thoughts and judgements that flows through our minds.

Letting Go of Attachments:

Meditation teaches us to detach from our thoughts and emotions. Instead of getting caught up in a cycle of self-criticism or rumination, we learn to witness our inner experiences with curiosity and compassion. This detachment allows us to recognize that thoughts are transient and do not define our identity or worth.

Embracing Imperfection

Through meditation, we come to understand that the human experience is only reflective of our conditioning and indoctrination, and is thus inherently imperfect. We all have flaws, make mistakes, and experience negative emotions. Instead of resisting or denying these aspects of ourselves, meditation encourages us to accept them as part of being human. This acceptance is not resignation but a willingness to acknowledge our imperfections and work with them positively.

Reducing Stress and Anxiety

By adopting a non-judgemental attitude during meditation, individuals can reduce the stress and anxiety associated with constantly evaluating themselves and their experiences. This acceptance of the present moment, without trying to change it or escape it, can be profoundly calming and reassuring.

Enhancing Self-Compassion

Meditation fosters self-compassion, which involves treating ourselves with the same kindness and understanding that we would offer to a friend in times of struggle. When we accept ourselves without judgement, we are better equipped to extend this compassion to others. It creates a ripple effect of empathy and understanding in our relationships.

Cultivating Resilience

The non-judgemental attitude of acceptance cultivated through meditation helps build emotional resilience. When faced with challenges or setbacks, individuals who have practised meditation are often better equipped to manage their reactions and bounce back from adversity. They approach difficulties with equanimity and a clearer perspective.

Living In the Present

Meditation trains us to live in the present moment rather than dwelling on the past or worrying about the future. This focus on the here and now can lead to greater enjoyment of life and a deeper appreciation of everyday experiences.

In summary, meditation is a transformative practice that teaches us to embrace a non-judgemental attitude of acceptance. By observing our thoughts and emotions without judgement, we become more self-aware, compassionate, and resilient individuals. This mindset shift can lead to reduced stress, enhanced well-being, and a more profound connection with ourselves and others. Ultimately, meditation empowers us to approach life with greater equanimity and acceptance, even in the face of its inherent imperfections.

Chapter Nine

SOME RESEARCH ON THE BENEFITS OF MEDITATION

1. Reduced Reactivity to Stress

Numerous research studies have indicated that engaging in meditation can enhance one's ability to cope with stress. While individuals still recognize stress-inducing stimuli, their stress response (commonly known as fight or flight) is diminished, resulting in a less severe impact from stressful situations.

Several theories have been put forth to explain this decrease in stress levels. One such explanation involves a decline in activity within the right amygdala, a region of the brain associated with triggering the fight or flight response. Multiple studies have established a connection between meditation practice and reduced activity in the right amygdala. For instance, in a study conducted by Leung et al. (2017), participants who practised meditation exhibited significantly lower anxiety levels and right amygdala activity when exposed to negative images, as compared to the control group.

2. Enhanced Emotional-Cognitive Functioning

Ellingsen and Holen (2008), Lutz et al. (2008), and Davidson (2010) have proposed that meditation techniques allowing thoughts, emotions, memories, and images to pass without judgement or suppression can eventually alleviate stress by fostering heightened awareness and acceptance of our emotions, without the need for stringent control.

According to the findings from Jian Xu et al.'s (2014) research, a connection was established between practising nondirective meditation (letting the mind freely wander) and heightened activation of the default mode network, a region in the brain associated with sporadic memories and the processing of emotions.

In simpler terms, this implies that when you allow your mind to wander during meditation, you engage in a significantly elevated level of cognitive and emotional processing, surpassing what occurs during periods of sleep.

The improvement in emotional processing is often cited as a plausible explanation for the psychological well-being benefits observed in those who meditate (Roemer et al., 2015).

3. Reduced Workplace Stress and Enhanced Job Satisfaction

The outcomes of a study conducted by Walsh et al. (2019) titled 'Effects of a Mindfulness Meditation App on Work Stress and Well Being' demonstrated that regularly listening to guided meditation recordings through the Headspace app for eight weeks had a positive impact on the well-being and distress levels of middle-aged individuals in a work setting.

Specifically, engaging in short guided mindfulness meditation sessions resulted in improved overall well-being, daily positive emotions, reduced anxiety and depressive symptoms, decreased job strain, and increased workplace social support when compared to receiving minimal education on stress reduction. The improvements in well-being, depressive symptoms, and job strain were sustained for two months following the completion of the intervention.

Other studies have corroborated these findings and suggested that practising mindfulness may contribute to a heightened sense of control over one's job by enhancing self-efficacy in handling work-related demands (Loucks et al., 2015), improving attentional control (Jha et al., 2015), and regulating emotional responses to stressful situations.

Anything that helps you connect with that inner source of peace and well-being is good. However, we must remember that any external object or idea that seems to give inner satisfaction is illusory and can be compared to a crutch for walking. As long as we use the crutch, we are not truly walking.

4. Enhanced Social Bonds

Recent findings indicate a connection between engaging in meditation and a rise in prosocial behaviour, characterized by actively assisting individuals experiencing pain or distress (Condon et al., 2013; Lim et al., 2015). The cultivation of compassion towards others may serve as the underlying mechanism through which mindfulness meditation fosters improved social connections and support (Cosley et al., 2010).

5. Of the Measurable And Immeasurable

We've all seen people running around evangelizing about meditation. If you dig deep enough, you can find 'studies' claiming that meditation can do all sorts of wonderful things: reverse your biological ageing, rest your mind and body, help curb your chocolate cravings, make you drive better, give you mind-blowing sexual experiences, and increase your chances of winning the lottery.

While a few may be true, most of these are just frivolous claims from unverified 'research' designed to be clickbait for cheap content. They serve only to lower the value and power of meditation while trivializing even some good research work. On the other hand, the problem with even serious research is that it's not possible to factor in all of the variables that are involved in a particular study, especially when psychological and even spiritual outcomes have to be quantified.

Here's one study that has measured only physiological parameters that can be measured and quantified. This study has been cited numerous times in meditation and sports circles. In meditation circles, it is cited by the so-called wellness and self-help gurus who try and inspire people to meditate while listing the benefits of meditation. In sports circles, it is cited by sports coaches to help improve the performance of their wards.

It involves meditators showing up to a lab room and getting connected to electrodes. Imagine as someone who meditates, you show up to this lab and they have you take off your clothes and put on a hospital gown. They sit you down in a chair. It's a steel folding chair and it has a hole in it. Then they connect electrodes to your scalp. They put a gas mask over your nose and mouth, and connect it to a gas analysis machine to measure oxygen consumption. They put an ocular gram on your eye to measure eye movement and a reference point on your earlobe. Next, they put a cardiogram on your heart to measure heart rate activity and then they stick a catheter in your arm to take blood samples.

In the palm of your other hand, they put a galvanic skin response device to measure how much you sweat. Then you feel some petroleum jelly underneath your butt, and they take a little thermometer and slide that up into you. It's to measure body temperature because all your other orifices are being used for some other kind of measurement. After all this, finally, they tell you to relax and meditate. Of course, everybody in that study reported having a horrible meditation experience. You and I too would have.

Now comes the strangest and most interesting bit! When they read the meta-analysis from that study, the physiological results reflected very positive changes. They ended up coining a term for this study: the relaxation response.

Chapter Ten

MEDITATION: BEYOND SCIENCE AND QUESTIONNAIRES

Psychologists and neuroscientists have made significant strides in understanding the cognitive and physiological effects of meditation. Nevertheless, its profound nature transcends the boundaries of empirical study. Meditation is a practice that leads to introspection and personal growth. That experience can barely be captured by questionnaires or scientific methodologies alone.

Meditation is not just a subject of scientific investigation but a personal journey that encompasses subjective experiences, personal growth, and spiritual dimensions. Let us explore the profound nature of meditation, emphasizing why its true essence can only be grasped through direct practice and personal exploration, and why science, with all its empirical evidence, may never fully explain it.

The Scientific Lens: A Glimpse into Meditation's Effects And Benefits

Before we get into the profound dimensions of meditation, let us acknowledge the contributions of psychologists and neuroscientists. Their research has provided insights into the effects and benefits of meditation on the human mind and body. These are validations of what many individuals who practise meditation have been saying for long.

- **Stress reduction:** Empirical studies have consistently shown that meditation can significantly reduce stress and anxiety. It achieves this by calming the mind, lowering stress hormone levels (such as cortisol), and promoting a state of relaxation.
- **Enhanced cognitive abilities:** Meditation practices have been linked to improved cognitive functions, such as attention, memory, and decision-making. These enhancements in cognitive abilities have practical applications in various aspects of day-to-day life.
- **Emotional regulation:** Meditation equips individuals to better manage their emotions. By fostering self-awareness and emotional intelligence, meditation enables practitioners to respond to emotional triggers with greater control and equanimity.
- **Improved mental health:** Scientific research has established a connection between meditation and improved mental health outcomes, including reduced

symptoms of depression and anxiety, and an increased overall sense of well-being.

- **Brain changes:** Neuroscientists have used advanced brain imaging techniques to observe the structural and functional changes in the brain that occur as a result of meditation. These changes include alterations in brain regions associated with memory, self-awareness, and emotional regulation.

Even though scientific findings are invaluable in highlighting the practical benefits of meditation, they only scratch the surface and provide a peripheral glimpse into the profound nature of this ancient practice. Meditation is not solely a technique for stress reduction or improvement of cognitive abilities. It is a journey into the depths of consciousness and self-awareness. The true essence of meditation goes way beyond the measurable outcomes of scientific inquiry. Regular and consistent meditation leads to experiences that are deeply personal and profoundly transformative.

The Subjective Experience: Beyond Measurable Metrics

At its core, meditation is an exploration of the self—a journey into the subjective scape of one's consciousness. It is an intimate experience that goes beyond what can be measured or quantified, and it is in this subjective realm that the true essence of meditation resides.

- **Self-discovery:** Through meditation, individuals embark on a voyage of self-discovery. It is a process of peeling away the layers of conditioning and societal influences to uncover one's true nature. This intimate journey leads to a deep sense of self-awareness and self-acceptance.

- **Inner peace and tranquillity**: The serene calmness experienced by individuals who meditate cannot be adequately captured through scientific instruments and data points. It is a state of being that allows individuals to find space and refuge from the chaos of the external world and access an inner fountain of peace and tranquillity.
- **In the here and now**: Meditation encourages a profound connection to the present moment and brings the focus of attention to what is often called the 'here and now'. Practicing individuals realize the futility of regrets about the past and worries about the future, leading to a fuller and more enriching experience of life by being in the here and now.
- **Spiritual dimensions**: The spiritual dimensions of meditation extend beyond the realm of science. The practice of regular and consistent meditation stimulates a sense of interconnectedness with all life. This feeling of unity with the universe inspires a deep reverence for the mysteries of existence.
- **Embracing impermanence**: Meditation leads individuals to a profound understanding that all things are impermanent and change is the nature of all things—that change is the only constant. This realization brings in a certain sense of liberation and freedom. It allows one to release attachments and embrace change with equanimity.

Such subjective experiences are the heart and soul of meditation. Scientific studies can provide evidence of the benefits of meditation, but they cannot fully capture the depth of these personal experiences.

The Transformative Power of Meditation

Personal growth: Meditation is not merely a relaxation technique; it is a transformative journey. It offers the potential for overwhelming personal growth and development that extends far beyond what can be achieved through any other means.

Self-reflection and self-improvement: Through meditation, individuals gain a heightened sense of self-awareness. This self-awareness becomes a catalyst for self-improvement as individuals recognize and address their limitations, biases, and destructive habits.

Enhanced creativity: Meditation has been linked to increased creativity. Quietening the mind and allowing space for new ideas to emerge often leads to innovative thinking and problem-solving.

Empathy and compassion: A natural outcome of meditation practices is heightened empathy and compassion for oneself and others. This heightened sense of empathy leads to more harmonious relationships and a greater sense of interconnectedness with the world.

Resilience and adaptability: Meditation naturally equips individuals to navigate life's challenges with greater resilience. It teaches the art of surrendering to what cannot be controlled and finding strength in adversity.

Clarity of purpose: Through meditation, individuals often gain clarity about their life's purpose and values. This clarity can lead to more intentional decision-making and a greater sense of fulfilment.

The power of meditation to transform lies in its ability to facilitate personal growth on multiple levels. It is a journey of self-discovery and self-improvement that empowers individuals to become the best versions of themselves.

The Spiritual Dimensions of Meditation: A Path to The Divine

Beyond the realm of science and personal growth, meditation offers a path to explore the spiritual dimensions of human existence. Regular and consistent practice of meditation helps us find universal and deep spiritual roots that encourage us to embark on a journey of deep connectedness and transcendence.

- **Transcendence and oneness:** Meditation practices aim to transcend the ego and the sense of a separate individual self. In these states, individuals report feelings of oneness with all of existence, a merging with universal consciousness, and a deep sense of peace.
- **Mystical experiences:** Meditation opens the door to mystical experiences that defy logical explanations. These experiences inspire an intense sense of the

sacrosanct nature of all life and provide a direct, personal experience of the divine.

- **Awakening and enlightenment:** Meditation is a path to awakening or enlightenment. It is a process of overwhelming transformation in which individuals realize their true nature and the interconnectedness of all life.
- **Inner guidance:** Through regular and consistent meditation, individuals receive inner guidance, insights, and intuitive wisdom. This inner wisdom can serve as a source of sagacious guidance in one's life journey.

It's essential to understand that the spiritual dimensions of meditation are deeply personal and can vary widely among individuals. What is universally recognized, however, is that meditation can serve as a bridge to the sacred and the transcendent, offering a direct and personal connection to the mysteries of existence.

The Unexplainable Essence of Meditation

Thus, while psychologists and neuroscientists have contributed to our understanding of meditation, its deepest nature remains elusive to scientific study and scrutiny. Meditation is a multifaceted practice that encompasses subjective experiences, personal growth, and spiritual dimensions that can only be fully comprehended through direct practice, experience, and personal exploration. It is a journey inwards, an exploration of the self, and a path toward inner peace and self-discovery that goes beyond what science can ever explain. Meditation's true essence lies in the transformative potential it offers, allowing individuals to embark on a deeply personal and profound journey of self-realization and spiritual awakening. It is an invitation to experience the unexplainable, to explore the depths of consciousness, and to connect with the profound mysteries of existence, one breath at a time.

Chapter Eleven

TRUE GRATITUDE: BEYOND NEUROLOGY AND PSYCHOLOGY, THE ESSENCE OF DEEP UNDERSTANDING AND MEDITATION

Gratitude is an emotion often associated with feelings of appreciation and thankfulness.

In a world dominated by scientific inquiry and empirical evidence, the idea that true gratitude is inspired by deep understanding gained through meditation may seem abstract or elusive. However, this perspective invites us to explore the depths of human consciousness and the potential for transformation that lies within.

While neurology and psychology offer insights into the mechanisms of gratitude and its benefits, they do not capture the essence of genuine gratitude that arises from a profound shift in perception. Meditation, as a practice that ushers in self-awareness, interconnectedness, and compassion, provides a pathway to this deeper understanding.

What started as an exercise towards being positive, for those who saw the cup as half empty, has now become a subject of academic research. Neuroscientists and psychologists claim to have made progress in understanding the neurological and psychological foundations of being positive by expressing feelings of appreciation and thankfulness. Studies have demonstrated that the act of expressing appreciation and thankfulness triggers the activation of specific brain regions connected to feelings of reward and social connection, such as the prefrontal cortex and the anterior cingulate cortex. Additionally, the release of neurotransmitters like dopamine and serotonin contributes to the positive emotions associated with this appreciation and thankfulness. The emotion behind the act of appreciation and thankfulness is termed gratitude. To 'cultivate' this emotion of gratitude, psychologists have also devised gratitude-based interventions, like gratitude journaling, which encourages individuals to record things they appreciate. These interventions have also been associated with heightened well-being, decreased stress levels, and enhanced interpersonal relationships.

While these findings shed light on the mechanisms of gratitude, they often emphasize its surface-level effects without delving into the deeper spiritual and philosophical aspects. True gratitude, as suggested by some traditions with a rich history of meditation, goes beyond mere neurological processes and external behaviours.

While interventions promoting gratitude have displayed positive effects, an ongoing debate questions whether these methods genuinely nurture authentic gratitude or merely foster a habit of politeness and thankfulness. The central issue revolves around whether these techniques can penetrate the very core of an individual's being and fundamentally alter their outlook on life.

Neurologists and psychologists typically concentrate on modifying outward behaviours and thought patterns, assuming that genuine gratitude will thus emerge. In contrast, advocates of the meditation-inspired perspective contend that this approach overlooks the true essence of gratitude. They propose that a profound shift in understanding and perception is achievable only through regular and consistent meditation, which inspires deeper-than-surface-level thoughts and actions.

Meditation has been a foundational practice in spiritual traditions for centuries. It involves observing thoughts without judgement and delving into the essence of consciousness. Through meditation, people have the opportunity to nurture self-awareness, gain profound insights into the fabric of reality, and cultivate a deeper understanding of their existence.

Meditation empowers individuals to forge a connection with their inner selves. A connection that transcends the constant chatter of daily thoughts. This connection permits them to explore the intricate interplay of emotions, thoughts, and perceptions, leading to a more profound grasp of both the self and the world. Within this state of profound realization and understanding, the seeds of authentic gratitude find fertile ground. Meditation helps individuals transcend the limitations of the ego, allowing them to experience a broader sense of identity that extends beyond personal desires and attachments. In this state, gratitude emerges as a natural response to the beauty and complexity of existence.

True gratitude is a state of being that arises when one recognizes the interconnectedness of all life and experiences. This recognition is not intellectual; it is a visceral realization beyond words. It is an understanding that everything is interconnected and each experience, whether pleasant or challenging, contributes to the tapestry of life.

In the serenity of meditation, we find solace in the tapestry of interconnectedness that threads through our existence. As the meditative practice becomes a steadfast companion, it gently peels off the layers of conditioning and preconceived notions that shroud our perception. What emerges is not merely a revelation, but a profound truth—a truth that instils in us an overwhelming sense of humility and awe. In this sacred state, we stand humbled by the boundless mysteries of existence, and our hearts resonate with gratitude that transcends the ordinary. It is not a mere catalogue of blessings, but a sincere appreciation for the very gift of life, for each breath that animates our being. True and genuine gratitude, born from the depths of our souls, becomes a testament to our recognition of the vast and wondrous tapestry of existence, forever reminding us of the preciousness of each moment we are granted in this grand symphony of life.

When we express such genuine gratitude, the true meaning of 'grace' dawns on us. Grace is like divine intervention, a loving hand reaching out to help us, to ease our burden and distress. Life then becomes a joyful experience and not one marked by suffering.

REFERENCES

Chapter One - MEDITATION: Busting Concepts

The Ashtanga yoga founder, Sage Patanjali penned the Yoga Sutras around 500 BC.
https://www.britannica.com/topic/Yoga-philosophy

Chapter Two - Taming the Monkey Mind

2{a} Stress signalling pathways that impair prefrontal cortex structure and function
https://www.ncbi.nlm.nih.gov/pmc/articles/PMC2907136/#:~:text

2{b} 10 Exercises for Your Prefrontal Cortex
https://heartmindonline.org/resources/10-exercises-for-your-prefrontal-cortex#:~:text

2{c} Facing the role of the amygdala in emotional information processing
https://www.pnas.org/doi/10.1073/pnas.1219167110#core-r4

EXPLODING MYTHS

Chapter Four - I Cannot Suppress My Thoughts

The Ironic Process Theory?
https://www.gloveworx.com/blog/ironic-process-theory/

Daniel M. Wegner famous for 'thought suppression'
https://news.harvard.edu/gazette/story/2013/07/daniel-m-wegner/

This is your brain on meditation: Brain processes more thoughts, feelings during meditation.
https://www.sciencedaily.com/releases/2014/05/140515095545.htm

Acem meditation
https://en.wikipedia.org/wiki/Acem_Meditation

(Book) The Power of the Wandering Mind
https://dyadepress.acem.com/allobjects/acemproduct/the_power_of_the_wandering_mind_nondirective_meditation_in_science_and_philosophy

Chapter Five - Prioritizing Stillness: The Art of Daily Meditation

Can meditation slow rate of cellular aging? Cognitive stress, mindfulness, and telomeres
https://www.ncbi.nlm.nih.gov/pmc/articles/PMC3057175/

How the ageing process works
https://www.theguardian.com/science/2009/oct/05/nobel-prize-medicine-physiology-2009

How meditation might ward off the effects of ageing
https://www.theguardian.com/lifeandstyle/2011/apr/24/meditation-ageing-shamatha-project

The study
https://docs.google.com/document/d/1Xzlu4F-KmcFH-rQK-7WYSAvEH2RuZpAjjpxNdL0lkRg/edit

Chapter Seven - The Illusion of Meditation as The Panacea

How meditation helps with depression
https://www.health.harvard.edu/mind-and-mood/how-meditation-helps-with-depression#:~:text

Chapter Nine - Some Research on the Benefits of Meditation

A Systematic Review of Associations between Amount of Meditation Practice and Outcomes in Interventions Using the Four Immeasurable Meditations
https://www.frontiersin.org/articles/10.3389/fpsyg.2017.00141/full

Enhanced Emotional Cognitive Functioning
https://www.ncbi.nlm.nih.gov/pmc/articles/PMC3935386/

Nondirective meditation activates default mode network and areas associated with memory retrieval and emotional processing
https://pubmed.ncbi.nlm.nih.gov/24616684/

Mindfulness and Emotion Regulation
https://www.researchgate.net/publication/273486003_Mindfulness_and_Emotion_Regulation

Reduced Workplace Stress and Enhanced Job Satisfaction
https://www.ncbi.nlm.nih.gov/pmc/articles/PMC6329416/

Enhanced Social Bonds
https://www.ncbi.nlm.nih.gov/pmc/articles/PMC4331532/

Support (Cosley et al, 2010).
https://www.researchgate.net/publication/247331693_Is_compassion_for_others_stress_buffering_Consequences_of_compassion_and_social_support_for_physiological_reactivity_to_stress

They called it the relaxation response.
https://journals.plos.org/plosone/article?id=10.1371/journal.pone.0062817